WHEELS ON THE BUS

Raffi Songs to Read®

WHEELS ON THE BUS

Illustrated by
Sylvie Kantorovitz Wickstrom

Crown Publishers, Inc. New York

Library of Congress Cataloging-in-Publication Data
Raffi.   Wheels on the Bus.
Summary: As the rickety old bus collects an odd assortment of passengers in a
quaint little town, the reader may join in with the sounds of the bus and motions of
the driver and passengers.
   [1. Buses—Fiction]   1. Wickstrom, Sylvie Kantorovitz, ill.   II. Title.
PZ7.R1237Wh   1988   [E]   87-30126

ISBN 0-517-56784-9 (trade)   10 9 8 7 6
0-517-57645-7 (pbk.)   10 9 8

Originally published in hardcover in 1988.
First paperback edition: February, 1990

Front photo copyright © 1987 David Street
Back photo copyright © 1987 Patrick Harbron

The wheels on the bus
go round and round,

round and round,
round and round.

The wheels on the bus
go round and round,
all around the town.

The wipers on the bus
go *swish swish swish,*

swish swish swish,
swish swish swish.

The wipers on the bus
go *swish swish swish*,
all around the town.

The driver on the bus
goes "Move on back!

Move on back,
move on back!"

The driver on the bus
goes "Move on back!"
all around the town.

The people on the bus
go up and down,

up and down,
up and down.

The people on the bus
go up and down,
all around the town.

The horn on the bus
goes *beep beep beep,*

beep beep beep,
beep beep beep.

The horn on the bus
goes *beep beep beep*,
all around the town.

The baby on the bus
goes "Wah wah wah,

wah wah wah,
wah wah wah."

The baby on the bus
goes "Wah wah wah,"
all around the town.

The parents on the bus
go "Shh shh shh,

shh shh shh,
shh shh shh."

The parents on the bus
go "Shh shh shh,"
all around the town.

The wheels on the bus
go round and round,

round and round,
round and round.

The wheels on the bus
go round and round,
all around the town.

WHEELS ON THE BUS

Moderately

Traditional

Bb7   Eb

1. The wheels on the bus go round and round,

Bb7   Eb

round and round, round and round, The wheels on the bus go

Bb7   Eb

round and round, all a - round the town.

2. The wipers on the bus
   go swish swish swish...

3. The driver on the bus
   goes "Move on back!"...

4. The people on the bus
   go up and down...

5. The horn on the bus
   goes "beep, beep, beep"...

6. The baby on the bus
   goes "Wah, wah, wah"...

7. The parents on the bus
   go "Shh, shh, shh"...